ALL PUPS
Found Their
SPECIAL
PLACE

DIANA G. LANGENAU

ISBN: 1493618393
ISBN 13: 9781493618392

Library of Congress Control Number: 2013920586
CreateSpace Independent Publishing Platform
North Charleston, SC

In a cold northern land far, far away,

Lived two golden dogs who
romped in snow all day.

His name was Hush.
He was very powerful and strong.

Her name was Whisper.
She was sweet, graceful, and long.

They spent many hours together,
exploring the great outdoors,

Seeing bugs on leaves, birds in trees,
and a waterfall that roars.

They spotted deer in the woods
and a raccoon perched up high,

A school of fish in a pond and
a frog swimming by.

Beneath a blue moon on
a magical starry night,

Standing nose-to-nose, they knew
a family would be right.

As the days and nights passed,
their love, it did grow,

Until one happy day twelve pups
arrived all in a row.

And, oh, what a summer that dog family had!

Cuddling, wrestling, exploring,
all with Mom and Dad.

Then one cool day they passed a still pond,
sparkling and blue.

The pups looked at themselves and
decided exactly what to do.

For puppies are born to help and
give out lots of love;

They were given these special gifts
from Heaven above.

So the very next day stood those
twelve puppies in a row,

Just waiting for that special someone
to take them and go.

There was Boomer, Buster, Hiccup,
and Howler, leaders of the pack,

Then came Giggles, Growly, Jiggles,
and Jabber a little further back.

Snicker, Sniffer, Whiner, and Whimper
made this family complete.

Not a nicer, sweeter dog family
would you ever want to meet.

Boomer went with a man wearing
boots that were muddy.

This pup romped in the woods and
became a hunting buddy.

Then there was Buster,
who was really smart and kind.

One day he became
a faithful friend to the blind.

Gentle Hiccup laughed and
made a clucking noise.

She lived with older people
and brought them many joys.

Howler, however, was rough
and tough and loud.

He became a football mascot
and was very proud.

Giggles was awfully silly
and refused to quite grow up.

She went with a teacher
and became a nursery school pup.

Growly could look very mean:
grumble, rumble and bark,

So he became the guard dog
in a junkyard after dark.

A clown from a nearby circus
spotted the pup called Jiggles.

Under the big top, these two
brought many giggles.

Jabber loved water, wind,
rain, and even the fog.

A captain took him home
to become a boating dog.

Snicker just loved life
and everyone she met.

She went to the big city
and became an apartment pet.

Sniffer smelled everything
with his rather large nose.

He rode in a police car
wherever it stops and goes.

Whiner was Sniffer's neighbor,
just two blocks down the street.

She sat in a shiny red truck and
lived in a firehouse—how neat!

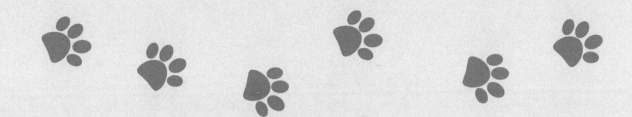

Whimper went home with a farmer
and learned how to gather sheep.

Then she laid on the porch,
looked over the field, and fell fast asleep.

As you can tell from this story,
all twelve pups found their special place.

Just look at their big brown eyes
and the smile on each pup's face.

Maybe you too can find
where your special talents might be.

Then take these gifts and
make a better world for you and me.

AUTHOR BIOGRAPHY

Diana G. Langenau is a dog lover who wrote *All Pups Found Their Special Place* while awaiting a new golden retriever puppy from a litter of twelve. Now retired, she enjoyed many careers, including teaching handicapped children how to swim, serving as a pre-school teacher's aide and working as an assistant in adult education. Her favorite job was being a Teddy Bear Technician when she helped each customer build their very own stuffed bear. She wrote this book from the heart, with the hope of enabling children to find their special place. The author has a loving husband, two married sons, and five grandchildren.

Made in the USA
Middletown, DE
06 May 2020